Holly Takes a Risk

Other titles in this series

Holly Takes a Risk

gillian shields

illustrated by helen Turner

BLOOMSBURY
CHILDREN'S
BOOKS

Map of

Coral Kingdom

Cauldron Cliff

Oceania

Giant Kelp
Forest

Rocky Islands

Fishing
Nets

Shipwreck

First published in Great Britain in 2006 by Bloomsbury Publishing Plc,
36 Soho Square, London, W1D 3QY

Text copyright © 2006 by Gillian Shields
Illustrations copyright © 2006 by Helen Turner

A CIP catalogue record of this book is available from the British Library

ISBN 0 7475 8768 X
ISBN-13 9780747587682

Printed and bound in Great Britain by Clays Ltd, St Ives Plc

1 3 5 7 9 10 8 6 4 2

All papers used by Bloomsbury Publishing are natural, recyclable products
made from wood grown in well-managed forests. The manufacturing processes
conform to the environmental regulations of the country of origin.

For Rhona, Sheena
and Catriona
— G.S.

This book is for my lovely grandparents
who have always encouraged me
to reach for the stars. All my love
— H.T.

Prologue

Meet Misty, Ellie, Sophie, Holly, Lucy and Scarlett. They are mermaid Sisters of the Sea, who live in the magical underwater world of Coral Kingdom. The Merfolk and their wise ruler, Queen Neptuna, look after the sea and all its creatures.

Coral Kingdom is protected by six powerful magic Crystals, which give life and strength to the Merfolk.

Without the Crystals, Coral Kingdom would not survive.

Every year, the old Crystals fade and have to be replaced. Queen Neptuna sends Misty and her friends – six special mermaids who are pure of heart - to fetch the new ones from the secret Crystal Cave. But as they are bringing the Crystals home, a storm blows the mermaids completely off course.

This is no ordinary storm! It is created by Mantora, Queen

Neptuna's jealous sister. Mantora wanted to rule Coral Kingdom, and now she is bitter and full of hatred. She is determined to stop the mermaids reaching home, so that she can overthrow Queen Neptuna and set up her evil Storm Kingdom instead.

Luckily, the young mermaids have courage and friendship on their side. But that's not all; their SOS Kits will help them as they race to get the Crystals back safely. And they never forget their Mermaid Pledge:

We promise that we'll take good care
Of all sea creatures everywhere.
We'll never hurt and never break,
We'll always give and never take.
And as we fight Mantora's threat,
This saying we must not forget:
'I'll help you and you'll help me,
For we are Sisters Of the Sea!'

Misty and her friends are eager to prove that Queen Neptuna was right to trust them with the precious Crystals. They are going to do everything it takes to get them home and safeguard Coral Kingdom for another year.

Will Mantora win? Or can the mermaids get the new Crystals back in time to stop the light fading for ever from Coral Kingdom?

Chapter One

The sun was setting in a blaze of gold over the sea. The mermaids Holly, Misty, Ellie, Sophie, Lucy and Scarlett had been swimming West with their new friends the dolphins. Earlier in the day they had rescued one of them, Silver, who had been tangled in a gill net. Now Silver and her sisters were turning aside to head for their home in the Wild Waves. They called 'farewell' to the mermaids by leaping high over the water in a shower of golden droplets.

'Goodbye, Sisters of the Sea!' called Silver. 'I'll never forget that you saved my life.'

'Thank you, mermaids,' cried her baby, Smudge, waving his soft flippers and

smiling with his snuffly beak. Then he
dashed happily after his mother, as the
dolphin family sped towards the far
horizon.

'It was exciting to swim with Silver
and her sisters,' said Holly, swishing her
yellow tail gently in the cool sea. 'But we
should rest now. We're all tired, and

Lucy can barely keep awake.'

'I can carry on,' said Lucy bravely. 'We must get closer to Coral Kingdom.'

Queen Neptuna had asked the courageous young mermaids to fetch six new Crystals for her silver Throne. If Holly and her friends didn't get them home by the end of the week, the power of the Merfolk would fade for ever. But Coral Kingdom still lay far ahead in the West.

'We can't swim on and on without stopping, Lucy,' said Misty, 'even though we'd like to.'

'Misty's right,' agreed Sophie. 'Tomorrow there will still be three days left before the old Crystals fade. Surely we can have a short break?'

'I think we'll have to,' yawned Ellie, 'if

we can find a place to sleep.'

'What's that ahead?' asked Scarlett, pointing in front of her.

Holly looked over the waves in the gathering dusk. She could make out some dark buoys bobbing up and down in the water, topped by flickering warning lights. Beyond them, a string of green mounds

rose gently from the sea in the twilight.
They were crowned by small, swaying
trees.

'It looks like a group of reef islands,'
Holly said. 'Those buoys are to stop the
Human boats getting too close. That will

be a perfect place to rest.'

'As long as Mantora isn't hanging around,' muttered Scarlett. 'Nowhere is safe whilst she's trying to stop us taking the Crystals home.'

The friends set off with weary limbs towards the reef islands. The moon sailed high in the sky and the sea sparkled silver. They swam past the bobbing buoys and saw the shape of the reef spread out below them in the clear, shallow water.

'This reminds me of Coral Kingdom,' said Misty. 'I think we really must be getting closer now.'

'Of course!' said Holly suddenly. 'I know exactly where we must be. And I know a story about these islands, an old legend.'

'Ooh, what? Do tell us, Holly,' cried the

others eagerly. They knew Holly was very clever and had learned lots of things about the ocean from Queen Neptuna's Sea Scrolls.

'Let's settle down for the night, then I'll tell you all about it,' she replied with a smile.

The mermaids quickly chose a small, deserted island with a soft white beach. They pulled themselves out of the water and sat in a circle on the glistening sand. Lucy found her Mermaid Comb in the dainty green pouch tied round her waist, and combed her friends' shining hair in turn. The cool night breeze ruffled their silky curls, as the stars began to glitter in the velvety sky.

'What about that story now, Holly?'

said Ellie drowsily.

'Yes please,' begged the others, stifling their yawns as they snuggled down to rest. They looked at Holly with expectant, sleepy eyes. 'Tell us a bedtime story, but don't make it a scary one!'

It was good to be quiet after such a busy day. Listening to a story reminded the mermaids of being at home with their families.

Holly smiled at her friends, took a deep breath and began.

Chapter Two

'These reef islands are called the Shipwreck Isles,' said Holly. 'I've seen them on Queen Neptuna's Great Map, which hangs in her Palace. Coral Kingdom lies beyond them, further to the West.'

'Why are they called the Shipwreck Isles?' asked Misty.

'That's all part of the legend,' replied Holly. 'You saw the coral reef under the waves. It's dangerous for the Humans to sail their boats too close to the sharp peaks and pinnacles of the coral, so there are warning lights on those buoys out there. But even so, there have been many wrecks in these waters.'

'I feel sorry for the Humans who are shipwrecked,' said tender-hearted Lucy. 'This sounds like a sad story, Holly.'

'The next part isn't sad at all,' Holly reassured her. 'It's about the most famous shipwreck of all, the *Lady Jane*.'

'That sounds like a fine, elegant ship,' said Ellie.

'It was,' answered Holly. 'The legend goes that the *Lady Jane* made her voyage here more than two hundred years ago. She had three tall masts, billowing white sails

and a splendid gilded prow. It was carved
in the shape of a…'

    '…a mermaid!' guessed Sophie and
Scarlett at the same time, laughing
together.

'That's right,' Holly grinned. 'The carved mermaid had a curling golden tail and long fair hair, but her sweet smiling face was a portrait of the ship owner's wife, the real Lady Jane. Her husband, Sir Richard, had worked hard to make his fortune in the prosperous lands near here. At last, he had sent his ship to bring Lady Jane and their children to join him in his new life.'

'So what happened?' asked Misty, with big, wondering eyes.

'A terrible storm sprang up as the *Lady Jane* reached these islands. The ship grounded on the reef and everyone's lives were in danger.'

'How dreadful,' whispered Lucy.

'Ah, but help wasn't far away,' Holly

continued. 'The Merfolk heard the pitiful cries of the young mother, and saw the golden mermaid prow plunging in the billowing waves. Lady Jane was clutching the ship's rails, with her children clinging to her skirts. She was weeping, saying that she didn't care if she sank to the bottom of the sea, as long as her babies were spared.'

'Poor lady,' said Ellie, 'how frightened she must have been.'

'Her gentleness and beauty filled the hearts of the Merfolk with pity,' added Holly. 'They rescued Lady Jane and everyone else before the ship sank, carrying them to these islands, where they were found safe and well the next day.'

'But what did the Humans say when they saw the Merfolk?' asked Misty. 'They must have thought they were dreaming!'

'The sailors babbled afterwards that a band of angels had snatched them from the storm,' laughed Holly. 'Of course, nobody believed them. But Lady Jane always declared that a mermaid had saved her children's lives, and she showed her gratitude in a special way.'

'How?' asked the friends eagerly. 'What did she do?'

'When she was reunited with Sir Richard,' said Holly, 'Lady Jane asked him to bring her back here on another boat. Then she cast her little ruby earrings overboard, as a thank you gift to the Merfolk. My granny told me that Lady Jane's rubies are still lying on the sea bed, near the ghostly wreck of her proud ship.'

'Ooh, how exciting!' said the others. 'That's a great story.'

'But is it just a story?' wondered Holly. 'Wouldn't it be amazing if we actually saw the *Lady Jane* tomorrow? We could even find one of the rubies and take it

home for Queen Neptuna!'

'The only things Queen Neptuna wants us to take home are the Crystals,' said Scarlett sensibly. 'We can't risk spending time looking for ghost ships, Holly.'

'But couldn't we just take a peep on our way home tomorrow?' Holly pleaded. Her head was full of legends and stories and treasure, so for once she wasn't being her usual cautious self.

'I suppose it would be fun to look,' said Misty. 'If you're really sure it won't make us late.'

'It won't!' promised Holly. 'We have to swim over the reef anyway, to head for Coral Kingdom. What do you all think?'

'Well, all right,' agreed Scarlett. 'But we'll have to get up extra early, so that we don't lose any time from our journey home with the Crystals.'

'I'll wake everyone as soon as the sun rises,' said Holly excitedly. The mermaids murmured goodnight to each other. Lucy began to sing a gentle lullaby in her sweet, soft voice:

> *Here is the end*
> *Of this bright day,*
> *Tomorrow we must*
> *Be on our way.*
> *But now we'll rest*
> *And meet our dreams,*
> *Beneath the stars*
> *And soft moonbeams…*

Soon the mermaid friends drifted off to sleep.

But Holly was restless. Muddled dreams raced through her head of ships and rubies and adventures, as the waves lapped all night long on the silvery shore.

Chapter Three

Holly thought she was still dreaming, when a wild sea bird cried out to greet the dawn. She opened her eyes sleepily. The pale light of the sun was starting to break through the soft clouds. Then she remembered. The mermaids were on the reef island and they were going to look for the wreck of the *Lady Jane*!

'It's the new day, everyone,' Holly

called, as she sat up.

The young friends slowly uncurled their sparkling tails and stretched themselves.

'We're heading for Coral Kingdom today,' Holly said excitedly. 'And who knows – perhaps we'll see the old shipwreck.'

The mermaids quickly got ready to leave. They checked that their magical Crystals were hidden safely in their pouches, and soon they were swimming out towards the reef, eager to be on their way. But Holly suddenly slowed down and looked around carefully.

'That's strange,' she said to her friends, as they rippled their bright tails through the fresh waves. 'Something looks different.'

'Perhaps that's because we're seeing the reef islands by daylight now,' suggested Ellie.

Holly hovered in the water for a moment, searching the waves with her keen dark eyes.

'Hmm, I'm not sure,' she said.

'Something has definitely changed since last night...'

'Are you worried, Holly,' asked Lucy, in a concerned voice, 'Should we stop?'

'Noooo...' Holly replied slowly. 'I'm probably just imagining it. Come on, we'll risk it. Follow me!'

She flicked her yellow tail and dived under the satiny sea in a splash of foam. Her friends swiftly followed. They were all thrilled by the sight of the magnificent coral reef, stretching out in the clear water below them.

'Oh, it's so like Coral Kingdom,' cried Lucy gladly. 'Look, there are turtles!'

'Parrotfish!' said Ellie.

'Shrimps!' said Sophie.

'Angelfish!' said Misty.

'And look at those gorgeous fronds of red seaweed,' said Holly. 'They're as bright as Scarlett's tail!'

The colourful coral was full of life. Some of the reef dwellers were just starting to wake up, and others were going to bed after a busy night. They watched curiously as the mermaids swam past, swishing their sparkling tails and making trails of silver bubbles.

'I wonder where we should look for the shipwreck,' said Holly, weaving in and out of the twisting branches of coral.

'Don't forget that we're just going to swim over the reef without stopping,' said Scarlett. 'We can't go out of our way for treasure hunting!'

'I know, Scarlett,' smiled Holly. 'I promise I won't do anything to put our Crystals or our journey in danger. I just think it would be fun to see the shipwreck – if it really exists.'

'If?' said a slow, deep voice behind them.
'If? Are you saying that you don't believe
the legend of the Shipwreck Isles?'

Holly and her friends whirled around in
the water. A large green turtle with a
dappled shell, strong flippers and a
comical face was eyeing them very closely.

'I beg your pardon,' gasped Holly.

'We've heard of the legend, of course, but we weren't sure whether it was real.'

'Of course it's real,' said the turtle sternly. Then he smiled. 'My name is Tobias. I have lived here many a year, and my family before me, going all the way back to the time of dear Lady Jane herself. I can show you the wreck of her ship if you like.'

'Can you really?' exclaimed Holly. 'That is, if it wouldn't take too long. We're on an important journey for Queen Neptuna,' she explained hurriedly.

'Well, well, we mustn't delay royal business,' replied Tobias. 'This will only take a minute.'

Holly looked at the others excitedly. 'Shall we?'

'Oh, let's go and see it,' said Misty. 'Just

a quick peek can't do any harm.'

'Then follow me,' said the turtle, gliding ahead of them in the clear water.

The young friends surged after him, curving round the spiky walls of the reef. After a little while, the strangest sight

loomed up below them. On the bottom of
the sandy sea bed, lying on its keel, was
the ghostly skeleton of a once splendid
ship. Its three great masts reached
upwards into the water, like slim trees in a
winter forest. The tattered remains of the
sails fluttered in the current, like a few
forlorn leaves.

'Oh, it's so sad and beautiful,' breathed
the mermaids. They swam closer and saw
the name LADY JANE picked out in
faded red paint on the wooden side. At the
front of the ship, the carved mermaid prow
still gleamed golden, though the face was
chipped and worn.

'So it was all true,' said Lucy softly. The
young friends gazed for a moment in awe
at the gallant, derelict ship, and thought

about the brave souls who had sailed in her.

'Was it worth coming to see?' asked Holly in a whisper.

'Definitely!' the others replied.

'I've heard that the Merfolk from the old times left Lady Jane's rubies lying in the sea nearby,' added Tobias. 'They said that mermaids would come back here to find the jewels one day. I don't know whether that part of the story is true. But at least you can see that the wreck is true, as real as you and me!'

'Thank you so much for showing it to us, Tobias,' said Holly gratefully, tearing herself away from the silent, shadowy ship. 'But we really do have to speed on our way now. Would you kindly lead us in the direction of Coral Kingdom?'

'Certainly, my dears,' he replied. 'It's been a pleasure to have some of the Merfolk by our reef once more.'

The gentle turtle led them up to the sparkling surface of the sea, just above the tips of the coral reef. Holly and her friends shook the drops of water from their shining hair and turned their thoughts to getting home with the Crystals. They listened carefully as Tobias gave them directions.

'To go West you need to follow…' the turtle began, but he never finished what he was saying.

A black cloud passed over the sun and everything went dark. Then a blast of icy wind whipped over the mermaids' shoulders and the sea began to crash menacingly around them.

'Something's happening!' cried Misty.

The waves suddenly swelled into green mountains of water, and out of nowhere a Human boat loomed over the friends like a menacing shadow. Tobias and the mermaids instantly dived under the huge waves out of sight, but not before Holly saw a man staggering by the wheel of the boat, desperately trying to regain control as the sea raged up and down.

It was too late. The bottom of the boat ripped against the sharp peaks of the reef with a sickly crunch. Water began to gush into it. Holly heard, hideous cackling laughter floating through the swirling wind and sea.

'Mantora!' she cried to her friends. 'She's here somewhere!'

Chapter Four

The boat lurched over on its side. Holly
and the other mermaids clung to each
other under the crashing waves. More peals
of triumphant laughter echoed around and
filled them with horror.

Above the freak waves the terrified man
was struggling to release the inflatable life
raft that was stored on deck. After a last
frantic effort, he managed to climb on to

the raft and get out of the way of the sinking boat. With trembling hands he sent up a bright red emergency flare. It blazed high over the sky, like fire from a volcano. All he had to do now was to wait for the next passing boat to find him and he would be safe, though with a terrible tale to tell.

A tremendous noise deafened the mermaids as the man's damaged craft finally tipped right over, sucked down into the churning sea. As it sank, six large, barrel-like canisters fell from the boat and knocked against the side of the reef. They startled all the fish from their hiding places like a cloud of silver butterflies. The canisters thundered down, down, down, and the boat landed with a heart-stopping

thump on the sea bed.
There was an uneasy
silence. The wind
and the waves
gradually returned
to normal. The young
friends looked around,
relieved that none of them had been hurt.
Tobias was quaking in his shell next to
them. The mermaids glided nervously over
the coral, peering down at the newly
sunken boat.

'Well,' said Scarlett, in a shaky voice,
'you wanted to see a shipwreck, Holly.
Now we really have!'

'It was horrible,' shuddered Holly. 'And
I'm sure Mantora was the cause of it,
trying to wreck our mission.'

The others murmured in agreement.

'I'm glad the man got away,' said Lucy, 'But why was he steering his boat so close to the reef? Didn't he see the warning buoys?'

'That's it!' cried Holly suddenly. 'The warning buoys! That's what was different when we set off for the reef this morning – they had gone. Someone must have removed all the buoys which told the boats to keep away from the sharp coral.'

'Who would have done such a thing?'
asked Ellie.

'Mantora!' replied the others, with a
groan.

'Let's think,' said Holly quickly. 'Why
would Mantora have attacked that
particular boat? What was it carrying?'

'I can tell you that,' said Tobias. 'Look
at those big barrels down there. The
Humans often take them far out to sea
and dump them. Then they lie forgotten at
the bottom of the ocean. But the barrels
are full of poisonous waste that the
Humans don't want on the land. It's
called chemi…oh, chemi-something…'

'Chemicals?' suggested clever Holly.

'That's the word I was looking for,' said
Tobias. 'The Humans aren't supposed to

throw these containers into the sea, but some selfish people do it all the same.'

Holly and the others peered down to where the shiny metal canisters lay on the sea bed near the wrecked boat. They had strange markings on them.

'Let's go and have a look,' said Holly determinedly.

'Be careful,' warned Misty. Then Holly turned to her with a very serious look on her face.

'I took a silly risk because I wanted to see the *Lady Jane*,' she said, 'but I'm not going to let anything bad happen to Tobias and the reef because of my mistakes. I don't trust Mantora one little bit and I want to see what she was up to.'

'We'd better come with you,' said Ellie. 'We are a team after all.'

Holly squeezed Ellie's hand gratefully, then swooped down to the sea bed with a flick of her yellow tail. The others swam near to her, with Tobias slowly following behind.

When the friends got closer to the metal containers, they could see what the marks

were. Two thick lines
formed an 'x' shape
with a round
blob in the
middle.

'The skull and
crossbones!' gasped
Scarlett.

'That's the sign for
poison and danger,' said Lucy anxiously.

'And it means that Tobias was right,'
explained Holly. 'These canisters contain
chemicals that the Humans wanted to
dump far out at sea. But they've landed
here by the reef because of Mantora's
cunning plot – and look!'

She pointed urgently at the heavy metal
barrels. Thin jets of black liquid were

escaping from two of them, clouding the
water with their filmy darkness.

'They're leaking,' exclaimed Misty.
'Those two containers must have been
punctured when they crashed against the
sharp coral.'

The mermaids peered down at where the
dark liquid spurted out. Both of those
barrels had a tiny round hole punched in
their metal sides. Sophie started to cough.

'This water is beginning to taste bad,'
she spluttered. 'The chemicals are spoiling
it already.'

'Move away, everyone,' shouted Scarlett.

Tobias and the mermaids shot away
from the wrecked boat and the canisters.
From a safe distance, they watched the
black liquid slowly seeping into the

beautiful clear water around the reef.

'If we don't do something soon to block up those holes,' said Misty, 'all the poison will escape.'

'And this part of the reef will die,' added Tobias miserably. 'Our beautiful red seaweed will wither away. There'll be no food for the fish and the other creatures. We turtles have lived here for so many years, but now our home will be destroyed!'

Holly looked at her friends with flaming cheeks, burning with shame. She bowed her head.

'This is all my fault,' she said. 'I'm so sorry.'

Chapter Five

'We don't think that it's your fault, Holly,' said Misty quickly, 'Do we, everyone?'

'Of course not,' soothed Ellie. 'Mantora might have attacked that boat even if we hadn't visited the *Lady Jane*.'

'I don't think so,' said Holly unhappily. 'She must have overheard us talking on the island last night and then planned all this. She's trying to stop us getting home with

the Crystals again. Oh, Scarlett, you
warned me that stopping to see the
shipwreck would be a risk.'

'I could have persuaded you not to, if I'd
really tried,' Scarlett replied ruefully. 'But
I secretly wanted to see the *Lady Jane*, too.
We're all to blame – or none of us!'

'It doesn't matter who's to blame,' said
Lucy. 'The important thing is how to stop
the black liquid hurting the plants and
creatures who live here.'

'And then getting back
on track with our
mission,' added
Sophie.
'You're right,'
said Holly, looking
at her friends' kind

faces. 'That is the important thing. Ideas, anyone?'

'Could we drag the canisters on to one of the islands?' asked Misty. The others glanced up hopefully. It seemed quite a good suggestion.

'I'm not sure that we'd be able to move them,' Sophie replied slowly. 'They look awfully heavy. And we don't want the poison leaking out on a reef island either. That could harm the crabs and birds there.'

'If we can't move those two containers,' said Holly, 'I think the best thing would be to block the holes up somehow. Then the liquid can't escape.'

'Good idea,' said

Sophie, 'but how can we stop them up?'

The mermaids eagerly searched through their SOS Kits, looking for something useful. Tucked away in a corner of her purple pouch, Ellie found a piece of dried seaweed. At the end of it was a small round pod, like a bead filled with air.

'Perhaps we could use something like this seaweed pod,' she said. 'Something small and round that would fit into the puncture holes.'

'A seaweed pod full of air wouldn't be strong enough, though,' Misty replied. 'It would have to be something hard and solid, something that was going to last for ever…'

'…something like a precious jewel,' interupted Holly with a shout. 'A ruby drop – Lady Jane's rubies!'

The young friends looked at each other with new hope.

'Do you really think we could find them in time?' asked Scarlett.

'The legend says that they lie near the wreck,' said Tobias urgently. 'That's what we turtles have always been told. I'll make sure that no creature swims near these leaking barrels, whilst you go and search for the rubies. Hurry, mermaids – and good luck!'

Holly led the way as the mermaids

surged back along the reef to where the wreck of the *Lady Jane* lay half-buried in the sandy sea bed. As they saw its eerie masts lying ahead of them, the determined young friends swept into action, searching all over the sea bed for the glinting jewels. But there was no sign of them anywhere.

'They must have fallen under the sand,' groaned Misty. 'We'll never find them in time.'

'We'll just have to examine every grain of sand,' said Scarlett stubbornly. 'We're not going to give up.'

Ellie and Lucy found some empty scallop shells in their SOS Kits. The mermaids used them to scoop up the glistening sand, then let it fall slowly through the clear water, trying to spot any flashes of red. But after scooping the sand over and over again, they felt discouraged.

'I'm afraid it's hopeless,' said Sophie. 'Even if we looked for a year and a day there'd always be another patch of the sea bed to sift through.'

'Then perhaps the answer doesn't lie there,' said Holly thoughtfully. She looked up at the ghostly rigging of the submerged ship. 'Maybe the rubies are hidden on the ship itself.'

The mermaids swam cautiously towards the grey hulk of the wreck. They drifted through the old masts and rigging, examining it carefully. Then Sophie

swooped down to the deck with a flick of
her orange tail.

'Look,' she said, 'we could get through
these broken deck planks into the ship's
cabin.'

The mermaids
peered through
the gaping hole.
It was very dark
inside, and silent.
They could just
make out strange shapes in
the gloom.

'We'll need our Crystals to give us some
light,' said Holly bravely. 'I'm going in!'

The others squeezed through the gap
after her, clutching their gleaming
Crystals. Glimmering light flickered round
the sunken cabin, and great shadows
sprang up and wavered on the walls.

'It's so spooky,' gulped Lucy.

'I think I've found something!' whispered
Scarlett. She shone her Crystal over an

ancient-looking chest in a dark corner. The
lid was studded with rusty iron nails and
was propped open slightly.

'That would be the perfect place to keep
long-lost treasure,' breathed Ellie.

The mermaids gathered round, their
hearts beating wildly, as Holly slowly
lifted the creaking lid...

'Aaah!' They all squealed in fright. A large, angry octopus shot out his snaky tentacles, startled from his slumbers in the old chest! The mermaids dashed wildly out of the dark cabin into the clear sea.

'Ooof!' gasped Misty with relief.

'I've never been so frightened in my life,' confessed Ellie, as the friends hovered by the wreck and watched the angry octopus swim away. 'But we must try to find the jewels.'

'I've just remembered something,' said Holly quickly. 'Tobias told us that the Merfolk in the old days said that mermaids would come back for the jewels at some time in the future. Well, what if those mermaids were actually us?'

'What do you mean, Holly?' asked Lucy in a puzzled voice.

'Some of the Merfolk are seers – they can prophesy the future,' Holly reminded her. 'Perhaps the mermaids who rescued Lady Jane could see that we would come along one day, needing her rubies! If they did know that, where would they leave them?'

'In a place where we'd look for her jewels,' murmured Lucy, with a strange expression on her face. 'Oh, of course…'

She suddenly darted towards the prow of the shipwreck, followed swiftly by Holly and the others. They clustered excitedly round the old carved mermaid. And there, on the cracked and faded head were…

'The rubies!' cried Holly. 'Lady Jane's statue is still wearing her earrings! Well done, Lucy.'

Holly reached forward carefully and unhooked the delicate jewels from where they dangled on the painted ears of the figurehead.

'Thank you, Merfolk of the old times,' she whispered. 'We came for the rubies, just like you said. And thank you, Lady Jane.'

Then the mermaids gasped. A trick of the light made it look as though the carved face smiled at them for a second.

'I think Lady Jane is pleased,' said Lucy softly. 'She wants us to have her jewels, to save the reef.'

'Then let's go and save it,' cried Holly. 'Swim back to Tobias with the rubies, everyone, before it's too late. *Mermaids SOS!*'

Chapter Six

The young friends swooped eagerly through the water, away from the old-fashioned wreck towards the new and much more dangerous one. Tobias was waiting for them with two other turtles under a ledge on the coral reef.

'These are my kinsfolk, Tara and Titus,' said Tobias. 'I warned them not to swim across this part of the reef until you had stopped up the leak. Did you have any success?'

'We found the rubies,' replied the mermaids triumphantly. They swirled to a halt and looked down at the broken boat. The dark jets seeping out into the water from the two punctured containers had grown stronger. A black cloud of gassy liquid hung over the wreck.

'I'll go down and try to fix the rubies into the holes,' said Holly bravely. Then she dived towards the ominous metal boxes, with the skull and crossbones on their gleaming sides.

'Wait,' called Ellie. 'You mustn't breathe in any of the bad water.'

But Holly was already

choking and spluttering, as she tried to get near the holes in the containers. She turned and sped back to her friends.

'I couldn't get close enough,' she coughed, her eyes red and stinging. 'But I have to stop up the holes or the poison will leak everywhere!'

A little crowd of worried creatures had gathered near the turtles, peering round the colourful branches of coral and the waving crimson seaweed. There was a squid, a family of boxer crabs and some brilliant blue-green parrotfish.

'What's that horrible black cloud?' they muttered anxiously. 'We've heard that the whole reef is going to be destroyed.'

'Stay calm, everyone. These mermaids are going to save our reef,' Tobias explained in a loud voice. 'They are being helped by Lady Jane herself!'

Relieved murmurs quickly rippled round the little throng, followed by, 'The mermaids are going to save our reef! They're going to save the reef!'

'*If* we can think of a way to get down to

the canisters without being poisoned ourselves,' whispered Sophie, looking over at the bright parrotfish.

'Parrotfish!' cried Holly, following Sophie's gaze. 'That's given me an idea. Parrotfish wrap themselves in a thick cocoon to keep themselves safe at night. That's what I need – a protective covering to keep me safe.'

'Take my silk handkerchief,' urged Scarlett, quickly searching in her SOS Kit.

Holly wrapped the handkerchief over her face like a mask, then dashed back down to the canisters. She dropped the glinting rubies into the holes with her nimble fingers. The jewels fitted exactly, and soon the hissing leaks came to a stop.

'Now we need to clear away the poison

that has already seeped out,' she called to
her friends. 'It's time to use our Crystals!'

The mermaids hovered at a little

distance from the cloud of discoloured water, holding out their bright Crystals. Brilliant red shafts of light, like tongues of flame, flowed from them and attacked the black liquid. For a moment there seemed to be a great burning ring in the water. Then the flames and the dark cloud of poison disappeared, leaving nothing but the beautiful clear sea.

Finally, Holly placed her Crystal on both the rubies in turn. They glowed a brilliant fire-red, like molten lava, then there was a flash of golden light.

'The rubies have been sealed in the containers by Mermaid Magic,' she declared to Tobias and the other creatures. 'Now they will never let a single drop of the black liquid leak over the reef. The red

seaweed, the coral, the fish are all safe —
and so are the turtles.'

'Hooray!' cheered Tobias and the others.
'We will cover this smashed boat and these
ugly canisters with sand. Then no one will
ever know that there was a new wreck at
the Shipwreck Isles. And,' he added, with a
twinkle in his eye, 'you mermaids have
proved that our legend is true.'

'I don't think I'll be searching for any

more ships from stories in a
hurry,' smiled Holly. 'It's
just too much of a risk!'
Then she looked serious
again.

'I'm so sorry, everyone,' she said, turning
to her friends. 'I'm glad we found Lady
Jane's rubies to save the reef, but all this
has meant a long delay to our journey
home.'

'Don't worry,' said the kindly green
turtle. 'We can show you the fast currents
that lead to your Coral Kingdom. You'll
soon be making up for lost time.'

'Oh, thank you so much, Tobias,' said
the relieved mermaids. 'You've been such a
good friend.'

Holly and the others hid their Crystals

away and swirled their sparkling tails.
Another long swim into the West lay
ahead of them.

The brave young Crystal Keepers were so
glad that Mantora hadn't been able to

wreck the reef, or their vital journey home. But the mermaids didn't know when or where she would be lurking next. It was going to take all their strength and courage to get the precious Crystals back to Coral Kingdom in time.

Holly took a deep breath and plunged after Tobias and the turtles.

'Come on, Sisters of the Sea,' she called. 'Let's go!'

Mermaid Sisters of the Sea

Misty has flowing blonde hair and a shimmering pink tail. Misty is a really determined and brave mermaid.

Ellie is very caring and loves sea birds. She has long, wavy dark hair and a glittering purple tail.

Sophie has funky fair hair and a blazing, bright orange tail, which helps her to swim super fast.

Holly has sweet, short black hair and a dazzling yellow tail. Holly is very thoughtful and clever.

Scarlett has fabulous, thick dark hair and a gleaming red tail. She can be a little bit bossy and headstrong sometimes.

Lucy has fiery red hair and an emerald green tail, but don't let that fool you – she is really quite shy.

By the same author